John Bliss

TIME WITH LEO

D1133415

John Bliss has written several nonfiction books for young readers, including *Art that Moves: Animation Around the World*, *Pioneers to the West*, and *Designer Babies*. His interest in science goes back to long summer nights of his youth, when he would lie on the front lawn, watching the stars through his father's binoculars. John teaches theater and communication at Northeastern Illinois University. He lives in Chicago.

First published by GemmaMedia in 2013.
GemmaMedia
230 Commercial Street
Boston, MA 02109 USA

www.gemmamedia.com

Printed in the United States of America

17   16   15   14   13   2   3   4   5

978-1-936846-36-8

Library of Congress Cataloging-in-Publication Data

{TK}

Cover by Night & Day Design

Inspired by the Irish series of books designed for adult literacy, Gemma Open Door Foundation provides fresh stories, new ideas, and essential resources for young people and adults as they embrace the power of reading and the written word.

Brian Bouldrey
North American Series Editor

GEMMA

Open Door

Inspired by the Irish series of books designed for adult literacy, Gemma Open Door Foundation provides fresh stories, new ideas, and essential resources for young people and adults as they embrace the power of reading and the written word.

Brian Bouldrey
North American Series Editor

GEMMA

Open Door

ONE

Now

Sam Peterson was not Popular. Not that he was terribly unpopular. Like many high school kids his age, his main goal was to make it through the day without being noticed. Not by his teachers, who were bound to ask him something he didn't know. (What was the deal with theorems anyway?) Not by the coaches, who might not try to humiliate him, but who managed to do so anyway. Not by the Popular kids, who treated him as if he had dropped a load in his pants. He had his circle of friends, who were pretty much like him, struggling to get by in a world they didn't create and didn't control. In his heart he knew high school wasn't designed to torture kids, but that didn't help. Things could be worse. He could be fat, or wear braces, or have over-active acne. There were millions of things that could lift you out of the inconspicuous middle and subject you to ridicule and scorn. Instead, he muddled along, happy when each school day ended.

If you had told Sam his whole life would change during lunch period, he would never have believed you. Lunch was an oasis in the storm that was daily life at Millard Fillmore High. At lunch he felt like he was part of a group. A ragtag collection of like souls was more accurate, but it was better than nothing. At lunch he could hang with his friends, have a few laughs, and, on a very good day, see Simon Snell squirt milk through his nose.

But lunch was when it happened, and Dylan Matthews was why it happened.

Now *that* wouldn't have been a surprise. Dylan Matthews didn't like Sam. Sam wasn't sure why. It was like Dylan saw him one day and thought, "I don't like this guy." From that day forward, Dylan made it his mission to bully Sam whenever he could.

Dylan was pretty lazy, and that applied to his bullying as well. He didn't shake kids down for their lunch money or give them swirlies in the toilet. He was big enough that he could probably pummel a guy pretty badly, and there were plenty of stories. Everyone knew *about* someone Dylan had beaten up, but no one ever saw it happen. For most kids, the threat was enough.

Sam's run-ins with Dylan consisted mainly of wedgies and chocolate milk shampoos. Dylan called him "squirt" or "Spammy" or, when he was especially fired up, "Shirley." Dylan was not particularly creative. Still, he was enough of an annoyance that Sam kept his distance.

Today, Dylan was the last thing on Sam's mind. Instead, he was deep in debate about the pros and cons of *Lizardman IV: Rigore Returns!* Danny Munch had the gall to suggest it was the greatest Lizardman movie *ever*, and Sam could not let that pass. In his excitement, Sam was on his feet, re-enacting a fight scene from *Rigore Attacks!* He spun around, ready for the final attack, when . . .

SPLAT!

Dylan Matthews.

Wednesday was Italian day at the caf, and Dylan had a double serving of spaghetti and meatballs. Rather, Dylan was *wearing* a double serving of spaghetti and meatballs. Sam had pulled out his invisible neutron gun at just the right time and just the right angle, and the rest was history. Messy, messy history.

The cafeteria went silent.

And then erupted in laughter. Even Dylan's sidekicks, Lurch and Burch (Lewis and Bertram, actually, but few people even knew their real names), couldn't help but howl in glee. Dylan's face went white, then red, and if smoke could have poured out of his ears, it would have.

"I'm gonna kill you, Shirley!" Dylan roared.

Sam was off. He was small, but he was fast. Years of dodgeball had made him flexible, and at this point, his fear was greater than Dylan's anger. The chase was on.

There was no place to hide in Millard Fillmore High. If Sam's time there had taught him anything, it was that. His best move would be to head to the office, but the code of kids everywhere was written in his DNA: "Don't Squeal." So he ran, with three pairs of feet thundering behind him.

Then he saw it: "Danger. Keep Out."

It was an ordinary door, just another

classroom. Sam didn't know what the Danger could be. He knew that Dylan and company wouldn't Keep Out because of a sign. But he was pretty sure that they would think that *he* wouldn't go into a room marked Danger Keep Out.

So he did. He opened the door, and dashed inside.

And then he was falling.

TWO

Then

THUD!

Sam was face down on a stone floor. He tried to pop up as if nothing had happened, but his body wouldn't respond. His head was spinning and his arms were rubber. The fall had knocked the wind out of him, helped in no small measure by the weight of his backpack. "Idiot, idiot, idiot," was all he could think. He had left the door wide open behind him, and Dylan and the Goon Squad were bound to be on him in a minute. With an effort, he sat up and caught his breath.

As he looked around himself, he thought, "Where am I?" He then thought, "That's what everyone says." But the question was reasonable.

The room was unlike anything he had ever seen at MFHS. It seemed to be a combination shop class, science lab, and art studio. The tables—there were several—were cluttered with paper and canvas and inkwells and . . . inkwells? Books were scattered around the room, and they were definitely old school. Their pages were uneven, and they were bound in leather or just tied together with cord. There were several paintings, mostly unfinished, and little wooden models of fantastic machines. The windows weren't the simple panes of glass he was used to, but were works of art—diamonds of glass enclosed by strips of metal. Some of the glass was colored, making the light seem alive. Some of the windows were open. The windows were *never* open at Fillmore— did they even open? But these windows were open, and the air was *different*. Fresher somehow.

"Well?"

The voice startled Sam. He hadn't realized there was anyone else in the room. He scrambled to his feet and said, "Sorry sir," almost out of habit. "I know this room is off-limits, but . . ." Sam's voice trailed off as he saw the figure in front of him. The man was old, but still full of life. His face was angular and surrounded by long white hair and a beard. He was dressed in a flowing sleeveless smock, which covered a loose shirt and heavy pants that barely passed his knees. Sam knew this guy—it was Dumbledore. "OMG I'm in *Harry Potter*," he thought. "How hard did I hit my head?"

"Don't just stand there. Did you bring the vitriol?"

"Excuse me?" Sam said. *Vitriol* was one of those words he had heard before but didn't know what it meant, and now that was going to bite him on the butt.

"The lead. For the ink."

Sam didn't know what to say. Dumbledore was looking at him as if he had three heads and none of them had a brain. "I'll just go back the way I came," he thought. Facing the Goons was looking more attractive. He turned to the door. It was definitely not the door he had come through. It was heavy and wooden, with a latch instead of a door-knob. He wrestled it open and stepped into the hallway. This was *not* Millard Fillmore High. The passage was long and dim, hung with tapestries instead of Emergency Evacuation Procedures. Sam's head was starting to spin again. He turned back and smiled weakly. "Where am I going again?"

"Oh, how he torments me!" the old man cried, raising his hands to heaven. He grabbed a brush and attacked the painting in front of him. It was a woman in a black dress. She had a slight but immediately recognizable smile.

A light switched on in Sam's brain. He knew the painting. It was the *Mona Lisa*.

Which meant the man wasn't

Dumbledore at all. He was Leonardo da Vinci!

But how?

"Excuse me sir," Sam said meekly.

"Go away! Tell them to send me a new assistant."

"I'm not your assistant," Sam replied.

"I know you're not. I just fired you."

"No, what I mean . . ."

"What! What what!" the man snapped at Sam. "What . . . what are you wearing?" For the first time, the old man looked at Sam. Really looked at him. "You are not from around here."

"No sir, I'm . . ."

"Quiet!" Leonardo studied him. "This hair. Very short." Sam drew back as the old man rubbed his head. "And this outfit. Strange. Definitely foreign."

Sam jerked as Leonardo reached out for him. "Stand still!" The old man was used to getting his way. He grasped Sam's jacket and rubbed the cloth between his gnarled fingers. "What is this material?"

"I don't know," Sam answered. "Some cotton-poly blend."

"Cotton Polly. I don't know her."

"Excuse me, Mr. da Vinci . . ."

The old man barked out a laugh. "Mr. da Vinci? Who is Mr. da Vinci?"

"I'm sorry, you look like Leonardo da Vinci."

"That's because I am Leonardo da Vinci! At least you know that much!"

"So Mr. da Vinci . . ."

"Enough! Mr. da Vinci is nonsense. I am Leonardo."

"I was just trying to be polite . . ."

"Polite has nothing to do with it. Da Vinci is not my name, da Vinci is where I am from. Where are you from?"

"Chicago."

"Never heard of it. It must be very small."

"No, it's very big. It's the third largest city in the United States."

"The United States! Ha!" Leonardo barked out another laugh. "The Italian states will never be united! Not as long as Florence wants to tear out the heart of Naples, and Bologna would trample Venice. Meanwhile Rome sits in the middle, puppet master to it all. No, as long as the Borgias and the Medicis and the Sforzas are constantly at war, Italy will remain a divided nation, joined only by the genius of Virgil and Dante. And Leonardo!"

The old man really liked to hear himself talk.

"No, you don't understand," Sam tried to explain. "The United States of America. America." Leonardo stared at him, question marks in his eyes. "Across the ocean. The New World."

Leonardo let out a laugh, a huge belly-rolling laugh. "Oh, you almost had me! The New World! 'Ah-mare-ee-kah.' Everyone knows the New World is home to savages and plant smokers. They say it is the land of men whose heads grow beneath their shoulders," he said, slapping his chest vigorously. "Mind you, I don't believe such stories.

But as a scientist, I must maintain an open mind. And as an artist . . ." He spread his arms wide, as if there were nothing more to say. "I like you, little savage. What is your name?"

"Sam," Sam replied.

"Sam. That's short for Samuele?" He pronounced it Sam-WELL-ay. "In any case, Mr. Sam from Chicago—in the New World," and he smiled when he said the words, "calling me Mr. da Vinci is like me calling you Mr. from Chicago. It makes no sense. Chicago is not your name, it is your birthplace. I am from Vinci, thus, Leonardo da Vinci."

Sam was surprised. "So you don't have a last name? Like Smith or Jones?"

Leonardo laughed with glee. "Do I look like a Smith? My full name is

Leonardo di ser Piero da Vinci. That is my name, my father's name, and the place I am from. What else do you need to identify a man? But I am called Leonardo, because there is only one!"

THREE

Proof

"So, my little savage, if you are not here to work, what brings you to Leonardo?"

This was a tough one. Sam thought he knew where he was, and definitely knew where he was from. But how he got from one place to the other was beyond his understanding. So he told Leonardo what he knew, and the more he talked, the crazier he sounded. Leonardo's face went from curiosity, to amusement, to amazement, to doubt, and back to amusement again. As Sam finished, Leonardo burst into laughter.

"A fantastical tale! It ranks with the

best of Homer or Dante. So young, and such an imagination. I envy you."

"But it's true," Sam insisted. "I don't know how it happened, but somehow I traveled here from 2013."

"And you came to Leonardo to send you back."

"I don't know why I came here. I just did."

"Fantastic," Leonardo repeated. "Hmmm. Your dress is certainly odd. Your rucksack," he indicated Sam's backpack, "is unlike anything I have ever seen. Still . . . this seems like a trick Salai would play on me."

"I know," said Sam. "What about this?" He pulled out his phone and showed it to Leonardo.

Leonardo took the device. "Interesting," he said. "A strange box. I don't recognize the material. This glass is very smooth." He stroked the screen and the phone came to life. With a shriek, Leonardo dropped the phone. "Demon!"

"No," Sam explained. "It's just technology. An advanced machine. You, of all people, should recognize that."

Leonardo poked at it. "What does it do?"

"You use it to call people. To talk to people far away."

"Show me."

Sam turned on the phone, and then felt foolish. It was a smartphone, not a time phone. There was no signal; there was no Internet; there was no one to call. Still, the phone worked, and all the information was intact. He made a few strokes, and then showed the screen to Leonardo.

"This is my family," he said.

"Amazing," said Leonardo. "So lifelike."

"It's a picture," said Sam. "From a camera."

"Like the camera obscura," said Leonardo. "But permanent."

"You know about cameras?" asked Sam.

"I invented the camera!" Leonardo showed Sam his drawings of the camera obscura. It wasn't a camera in any sense that Sam knew. It didn't take pictures. It wasn't much more than a dark room with a small hole at one end. The hole let in light, and the light created an image.

"But this," said Leonardo, "this is much more than I have ever imagined. Perhaps your story is true."

"Still," said Sam, "I don't know any way you could possibly get me home. No offense, but you're just a painter."

"Just a painter!" Leonardo roared. "The greatest painter! And the greatest inventor! I have been hired by Cesare Borgia—*Cardinal* Cesare Borgia—as his chief military engineer. If anyone can find a way to send you back, it is I."

With that, Leonardo started shuffling through his drawings. "Hmmm, let's see. I could use my giant crossbow to shoot you into the future. No, that would never work. And it would probably kill you. My mechanical man? Too slow, too slow." He continued to look through his papers, with the occasional "hmmm" or "aha!"

"No," he said at last. "This is a puzzle." His eyes brightened. "But where there is a puzzle, there is an answer. And if an answer can be found, who will find the answer? Leonardo!"

FOUR

Dinner

Time dragged on, and the light began to fail. The darker it got, the more Sam doubted he would ever get home. Leonardo lit candles, filling the room with a warm glow. But Sam's spirits continued to sink.

"Samuele, there is only one solution to our problem. Dinner!"

Leonardo rang for a servant, and soon the room was filled with plates of food. It had been hours since Sam had fallen into Leonardo's room, and he was starving. Somehow, the spread before them did make everything seem a little bit brighter. There was bread with herbs and salt and olive oil. It was like pizza, but without tomato sauce or cheese. There was plenty of cheese and sausages, so Sam made his own pizza. When he asked about tomato sauce, though, Leonardo was shocked.

"Tomatoes? Poisonous. Not even fit for peasants." By now, Sam had learned not to argue.

There were vegetables, and tiny chickens. At least Sam hoped they were chickens. And plenty of wine. Sam was surprised when Leonardo poured him a glass, but he didn't object. Soon, he was feeling much better. As was Leonardo.

"So," said the old man, "what else do you have in this magic sack of yours?" Before Sam could stop him, Leonardo emptied the backpack on the table. There were books and pens and snacks—nothing unusual. Leonardo stared as if it were a pile of gold. "Amazing. Amazing." He picked up the book and ran his finger along the pages. He turned the volume so the candlelight reflected off the cover. He opened the book. His eyes were wide and his jaw hung slack. "If Gutenberg could see this, he would die. Again."

"It's just a book, Leo." Sam's tongue felt thick.

"Leo? Like the pope? Or the constellation?"

"Sorry Leonerdo. Nudo. Nardo." Sam giggled.

"Perhaps you've had enough wine, Samuele. Leo is fine. I like it."

Leo turned his attention back to Sam's things. He picked up a yellow highlighter, and took off the cap. He touched the tip, then looked down at his finger. "A color stick!" Leo grabbed a piece of parchment and drew a line. "Marvelous!" One after another, he took Sam's pens and pencils and markers and sharpies and scribbled on the parchment. Sam joined in, and soon they were both laughing like children. Sam showed Leo how to play tic–tac-toe, which Leo conquered in no time. They moved on to Hangman, but gave it up when Sam played *television* and Leo countered with *risotto*.

"Leo," Sam finally asked, "do you really think you can get me home?"

"I don't know, little savage." Leo replied. "It's a challenge. But what is life without challenges?"

FIVE

Eensteen

The next morning, Leo was up and active long before Sam rolled out of bed. He stumbled into the studio, yawning and stretching and yearning for more sleep. "Good morning, little savage!" Leo sang out as he gathered books and papers and an assortment of equipment. "How did you sleep?"

"Surprisingly well," Sam replied, and it was surprising, considering that his bed was little more than a cotton sack stuffed with wool. Of course, his sleep had probably been improved by all the wine.

"Excellent! So wash your face and get dressed; we are off on an adventure."

Washing his face seemed to be the only option, as Leo's rooms didn't have a shower, or even a bathtub. Instead, Sam had to make do with a basin of perfectly cold water and a rough cloth. He washed as best he could, but when he started to get dressed, Leo stopped him.

"No, no, Samuele, your future clothing will never do here. I've laid out some things for you." The "things" turned out to be little more than tights, a loose shirt, a vest, and some sort of athletic supporter. Sam opted to keep his own underwear. Still, no matter how hard he tugged, the shirt would not cover his rear end. Leo did nothing but laugh.

"You think all the ladies want to see your bottom? Pah! After the glorious behind of Michelangelo's David, your scrawny butt is nothing to them but chicken parts."

"You're in a good mood this morning," Sam observed, to move the discussion away from his pants, or lack of them.

"That's because I've been reading your Eensteen. In that marvelous book of yours."

"Eensteen?"

"Yes! Eensteen says space and time are curved, like an orange, no?" Leo rotated his hands in the air, describing a globe.

"Oh, Einstein, yes." The fact was, Sam had made little sense of anything Einstein said. All he knew was that $E = mc^2$. Even then, he couldn't tell you what the equation meant, or why the two was up in the air like that. Leo moved on.

"Ah, Einstein. What he says makes sense, yes? Look at the natural world, everything is curved. The Sun, the Moon, circles everywhere. So Einstein says space and time curves back on itself, thus." And on *thus*, Leo slapped the palm of his left hand on the back of his right.

"Okay . . ." Sam replied. He wasn't sure where this was going. But that was true of most things that came out of Leo's mouth. Or Einstein's.

"And that, my friend, is how you got here! This," he pointed to his left hand, "is your time. And this," he pointed to the right, "is my time. And this," again he slapped his hands together, "is how my time meets your time. And you sneak through, like a mouse through a crack in the wall. You see!"

Sam did not see, but he was willing to accept what Leo was saying, especially if it meant getting home. "So where are we going?" he asked.

"Ah, this is where Leonardo comes in, and transcends Eensteen. Einstein! When you first appeared, there was a change in the air. A wind, a . . ." Leo wiggled his fingers in the air vaguely, "a smell. Something. I assumed it was the door. *But* . . . you did not come through the door! So what is the source of this phantom wind?"

Sam shrugged.

"It *was* the door. The door from your world to my world. And we will find it with this!" Leo waved a stick at Sam. Attached to the top were two crossed rods with a cup at each end. "It's my own invention. The anemometer. It measures wind speed!"

"And this will help us . . . how?"

"Observe!" said Leo, and he stood the instrument on a table. Nothing happened, and Sam said so. "Correct! And now, observe when we place it where you entered the room." Leo placed the device on the floor. Slowly, oh so slowly, the framework at the top began to turn.

"It's very weak here. It's been nearly a day since you came. But there is still a shadow of a force. And this is the force we will follow to track our door back to your world."

SIX

Outside

The next thing Sam knew, they were out in the street. Leo carried parchment and the anemometer. He had shoved some of Sam's pencils into his belt. Sam carried a sack with everything else. "Everything else" was more parchment, some pens, other scientific devices, and a lunch of cheese, sausages, and the ever-present wine. Sam wished he had his backpack, but even he had to admit it would probably attract more attention than was smart. He added his phone to the sack, more out of habit than anything else. Sam felt better knowing he had it with him.

The activity on the street was overwhelming. People were everywhere, and so were animals, carts, merchants, and soldiers. It was as if a Renaissance fair had been dropped into the middle of downtown, only with more mud, hay, and animal poop. Between the people, the pushing, the smell, and the sound, there was no way Leo could possibly get an accurate reading of air speed.

And yet, impossibly, he was doing just that. Leo seemed to know every doorway and alley, every nook and cranny in the city. Every few minutes he would duck out of sight and then emerge again, triumphant. Sam couldn't tell what Leo was doing, but he seemed very happy with the results. Now and then he would grab another device from the sack, and then return grinning, sometimes exclaiming "Excellent!" or "Grande!"

Slowly but surely they circled the building—which was more a palace than anything else—and then Leo struck out in one direction. Sam followed as best he could. Despite his age, Leo snaked through the crowd with astonishing ease. Fortunately for Sam, he seemed to know everyone in town, and every few blocks someone would take a minute of his time, giving Sam a chance to catch up. Unfortunately for Sam, this made it hard to remain unnoticed. But it seemed that Leo had had many assistants over the years, and outside of the occasional pat on the back or ruffling of his hair—which Sam loathed—no one paid him much attention.

Before long, they were out of the city and into the countryside. Here it was easier to see what Leo was doing. Not minding any existing paths or roads, he walked purposefully on his way, sometimes for a few minutes, sometimes for up to half an hour. Then he would stop and slowly spread out his arms, as if he were feeling for something. Sometimes he would pace, slowly, from side to side. Sometimes he would sniff the air. Then, when he found just the right place, he used the anemometer. It was hard to get a good reading out in the open air, so Sam blocked the wind. Occasionally Leo pulled another device from the bag and made measurements. Then he would nod his head and unroll the parchment. Sam saw that it was a map, very detailed and very accurate. Leonardo would mark the spot and continue a dotted line that connected all of his readings back to the spot where they started.

"That's a beautiful map," Sam commented. The words *beautiful* and *map* hardly seemed to go together, but in this case it was true. The map was drawn and colored by hand, and a tiny, spidery script indicated points of interest.

"Thank you," Leo replied. "It was the devil to make."

"Wait, what? You made that? You're a painter, an inventor, and a mapmaker?"

"And a poor poet, and a decent musician, and an excellent architect. And right now, more than a little hungry." With that, Leo laid back in the grass.

"Is there anything you can't do?" Sam asked.

"I cannot cook to save my life, and I'm terrible at managing my money. Fortunately, there are many wealthy men who are willing to pay me well for my talents. Now unpack our lunch."

"But shouldn't we keep tracking the door?" "Door" had become the accepted word for whatever portal connected the two time streams.

"The door will wait," Leo replied. "Lunch will not."

SEVEN

Art and Science

As they ate, they talked. Sam asked Leo about maps, and Leo asked Sam about high school. He was pleased that education was free and open to all. With some prodding, he even accepted the idea that women deserved to be educated along with men.

"Why did you decide to become an artist, Leo?" Sam eventually asked.

Leo smiled. "One does not decide to become an artist. One is an artist or one is not. My family wasn't wealthy enough for me to become a doctor or a lawyer. Fortunately, my father knew an artist who would train me. When I was about your age, as a matter of fact. Ah, Verrocchio. He taught me carpentry, drawing, and sculpting, and he gave me my first chance at painting."

"Look at those shadows." Leo pointed out the shadows cast by the leaves of the tree they sat beneath. "What do you see?"

"Shadows?" Sam replied, somewhat uncertain.

"Yes, but what do you see? Light and dark?"

"Sure. But no." Sam puzzled it out. "Some shadows are darker, and some are lighter. Some are very clear, and some less so. There are patches of light where the sun shines through. I don't know what you want me to say!"

"Ha ha! You just said it, Samuele.

Light. To be an artist, you must see the light. How it plays, and sculpts the shape of objects, and sometimes fools us. Shadows are never completely black. The light shines through, or rolls around the edges. Paints and brushes, these are nothing. Light is the ultimate tool of the artist."

Sam was suddenly struck. "OMG I'm talking art with Leonardo da Vinci!" *That*, he thought, was the ultimate Facebook status. Suddenly, he wished he were home. Would he ever get back? Maybe Leo *was* a genius, but time travel? They didn't even have that in Sam's world. It seemed hopeless.

"I'm scared." Sam finally admitted it.

"Scared? Of what?" Leo asked.

"That I'll never get home. That I'll

be trapped here. I'm afraid of what will happen to me, what will happen to my folks. I'm scared of everything!"

"Ha!" Leo barked. "You're not scared. Let me tell you about fear."

"Great," thought Sam. "Another story."

"When I was a young boy—much younger than you—I got lost in a cave. I was curious, so I went inside. There were so many twists and turns that I got lost in no time. Then my heart began to race. Were there monsters? Were there pirates?"

"Pirates? In a cave?"

"I was a young boy. You know what I found in that cave?" Leo paused, for dramatic effect. "Nothing! Just a dark, dank hole, covered in moss and lichen and crawling with bugs and lizards. And bats! Lovely, lovely bats. Have you ever watched a bat fly?"

"I don't think so," Sam replied. The thought of bats made him squeamish.

"That's because you don't open your eyes! Watch the bats. Less efficient than birds, always flapping, while birds soar. But much easier to reproduce. Thin leathery wings. Very clear structure. A little wood and cloth and you have a bat wing in no time. Simple."

"But I distract myself! The cave. From the outside, it's a mystery. A dark place, removed from the world we know. But inside the cave, it *is* the world. It has its own rules, its own light, its own life. Why do we fear the cave?"

"Because it's scary?" All Sam could think of was being surrounded by bats in a cave.

"Pah!" cried Leo. "What do we fear? Above all, what do we fear?"

"Spiders? Snakes? Falling? . . . Death?" Sam was afraid of a lot of things.

"No," said Leo. "We fear the unknown. Suppose you fear spiders. Then look at spiders, learn about them. Learn what they want, how they live. Learn to tell them apart, which ones are dangerous. You may still hate them, you may find them ugly. But you will not fear them."

Sam had no interest in studying spiders.

"You say you're scared. That's just because you don't know what's going to happen. I don't see a scared boy. When you fell into my room yesterday, you didn't run around screaming. You figured things out. You figured out that I was Leonardo, you figured out how to prove where you were from. This is not what a frightened person does. You're smart, Sam." Leo poked him in the head. "You just don't believe it."

Sam was surprised. People had called him many things, but "smart" was never one of them.

"Now then. Let's go find your door." And off Leo strode, leaving Sam to collect what was left of lunch.

EIGHT

The Door

And there it was.

Not right away. There was more marking and measuring, climbing through weeds and crossing streams. Leo plotted a course based on his observations, and bush or briar, they followed along. Leo taught Sam to feel the vibrations in the air, to pick out the faint metallic smell along the course the portal had traveled. Sam wondered why he hadn't noticed it before. As they walked, he noticed it more and more. It became stronger. His pulse quickened and his heart beat faster as he realized that they were close to his passage home.

And there it was. Sam could not only sense it, he could see it. A faint shimmering. A disturbance in the air. The Door.

"Leo."

"I see it."

They stood still, quiet, as if they were stalking a deer, as if the gap in time and space would run away if it sensed them.

"People are gonna freak when I show up in these clothes," Sam thought. Now he really wished he had his backpack with him. At least he had his phone. His books, his notebooks, even his clothes could be replaced. But his life was in his phone.

"Hey Leo, say cheese."

"What about cheese?" Leo scowled and raised an eyebrow.

CLICK

The light flashed as Sam took Leo's picture. Leo screamed.

"I'm blind! Monster, demon, what have you done to me!"

"It's just the flash, Leo! You'll be fine," Sam assured him.

"Oh," Leo said as his sight returned. "Sorry. You surprised me."

"See?" said Sam, as he showed Leo the picture.

"I don't like it. Too clear. No mystery. I'm not ready for your technology."

"Then this is goodbye." Sam hugged the old man, hard. "I don't know what I would have done without you."

And he was off. The door shimmered, calling him home. "Sam, wait!" Leo called after him. But Sam was thirty-five years younger and five hundred years faster.

The door grew closer.

Sam ran harder. He closed his eyes.

Until—SLAM—he was through. And still running.

"Samuele!" Sam could still hear Leo's voice. But that was impossible. Unless . . .

Unless it hadn't worked. How? How could it not have worked? It was his door. It was the way back. Leo explained it, and Leo knew everything.

Leo stood in the distance, his shoulders slumped. Sam felt like someone had punched him in the stomach.

"What happened? Why didn't it work?" Sam had been right. He would *never* get home.

"We need to open the door." Leo's voice was quiet.

"How do we do that?" Sam groaned.

There was a pause. A long pause. "I don't know."

NINE

Rebirth

By the time Sam and Leo got home, night had fallen. The streets were still busy, but Sam barely noticed. All he wanted to do was sleep. Maybe for five hundred years.

Lamps were lit in Leo's room, and as they neared, the door opened. Someone stood in the doorway. "My God, Leonardo, where have you been?" he said. "You look like hell. And who's the kid?"

The someone was a young man, a few years older than Sam. He was taller than Sam as well, with curly hair and a prominent nose. "Ah, Salai," Leo said. "You're back."

"Who's the kid?" Salai repeated.

"This is Samuele," Leo said. "He's staying with us for a while. Samuele, may I introduce Gian Giacomo Caprotti da Oreno. My apprentice."

Sam reached out his hand, but Salai barely acknowledged him. "So you've been out for a jaunt? Rolling in the mud by the look of it."

"We were out conducting an experiment." Leo looked as tired as Sam felt.

"You couldn't wait for my return?" Salai was used to getting his way.

"NO!" Leo spun and glared at the young man. "No, we could *not* wait for your return. I'm cold, I'm tired, I'm sick at heart. The last thing I need is your needling. One more word . . ." Leo stopped himself. "I'm going to bed. I expect you to treat our guest as a guest." With that, Leo turned his back and went to his room.

"So. Welcome, Little Prince." Salai bowed to Sam.

"Look, Salai—" Sam started.

"Don't even. My name is Gian Giacomo. You may call me Gian Giacomo. If I get to like you, you may call me Gian. Understood?" Gian Giacomo glowered at Sam.

"I'm sorry, Leo called you Salai," Sam said.

"Leo. Interesting. Well, *Leonardo* can call me Salai. It is his nickname for me.

Little boys like you call me by my given name."

"Sorry. Gotcha." Sam wished this day was over. He wished the whole visit were over. He wished he were back at home with the bullies he knew and loved.

"Let me explain something, Samuele. Leonardo picks up strays all the time. He's famous, he has his fans. Old, young, men, women. They chase him down and he loves the attention. They come, they go. I stay. When you are long gone, when Leonardo no longer remembers you, I will be here."

"I'm not planning to stay," Sam said. What he thought was, "If you knew how much I want to leave, it would make your head explode."

"Good," said Salai. "Remember, I'm

the main mozzarel. You are yesterday's curds and whey."

* * * * *

Sam didn't sleep nearly as well that night. Instead of the cozy bed—Gian Giacomo's bed, as it turned out—he slept on a sofa in the studio. It was comfortable enough, but not nearly long enough. He kept thinking of yellow Ned in his too-small bed from *One Fish Two Fish Red Fish Blue Fish*. It didn't help that Gian Giacomo snored. Loud. As did Leonardo. Whenever Sam started to drift off, a sudden snort or wheeze from one room or the other rocked him back awake.

Still, he must have fallen asleep at some point, because the next thing he knew Leo was up and banging about.

"I have the answer, Samuele, I have the answer. It comes to me in my sleep; it always comes to me in my sleep." Leo was perched on a stool at one of the tables, surrounded by parchment and drawings and Sam's science textbook. He had a plate of fruit: apples and pears, and others that Sam didn't recognize. Every now and then, Leo absentmindedly stuck his pen into one of the fruits—a persimmon was his primary target—but whenever that happened, he merely wiped it off and started again. Sam made it a point to avoid the persimmon. The rest of the fruit was amazing, though—sweet and fresh and unlike anything Sam had ever eaten at home.

"What's the answer?" Sam asked, looking at Leo's sketches.

"The answer, ah! It's obvious. The door is locked, and so we, we must unlock the door." Leo launched into a discussion of vortices and dimensions and relative space-time that was mostly over Sam's head. But the drawing was amazing. Something like a bicycle was attached to a cone topped with a curved ramp. The whole thing was circled by a couple of hoops, and it was all connected with gears and pulleys. Smaller drawings showed how everything went together, though none of it made much sense to Sam. Leo made notes to the left of the drawing, and he wrote everything backward—from right to left instead of left to right. Letters, words, everything was backward.

Sam had to ask. Was it code? Was it a way to keep his ideas secret?

"Oh no," Leo replied. "It's because I'm left-handed. I don't want the ink to smear. So this is the machine. The time machine. What do you think?"

"Will it work?"

"I have no idea. But it gives us something to do instead of just pouting about our bad luck, eh? Now where is that sluggard Salai? I need him to get some equipment. Salai, out of bed, you lazy mole!"

TEN

The Time Machine

The next few days were all about work. As rude as he was, Salai worked hard. He always knew what Leo needed, and was at his side before the great man called him. Salai worked the forge and shaped the metal parts, leaving Leo free to craft the huge canvas sheet for the machine, which he called his "aerial screw." This canvas was the spiral ramp atop the cone. It wasn't a ramp at all, but a sail. In Leo's new design, a rider drove pedals to turn the screw against the wind. Leo worked the fabric like a seamstress making a gown.

Sam's job was mainly to fetch and

carry. He didn't mind it. It gave him time to watch the two craftsmen turn wooden planks and rods of metal into an amazing machine. Sam took pictures, but only a few. There was no way to charge his phone, and he wanted to save what little power was left.

Leo's workshop was on the ground floor, and now and again a friend or admirer would come by to see what the genius was building. Leo was always careful to hide Sam away from prying eyes. To Sam it all seemed silly. He was just a kid, and everyone liked Leonardo. Leo wasn't so sure. "You must always be careful, Samuele. There are men here who would use you for their own ends. For the power you represent. For your knowledge."

"I don't have any knowledge, Leo. You have all the knowledge."

"Not so. You know the future! Your books have secrets unknown to my people. Things that are commonplace to you are miracles here. Knowledge is power, and many men are hungry for power."

Cesare Borgia visited often. He was tall and thin, with dark, piercing eyes. Sam thought he would make a good cop, or drug lord. Borgia was always dressed in the finest linens and furs, yet he still gave the impression of having crawled out of a sewer. His hair was long and limp and never seemed quite clean. His lips were just as long and thin and always carried a hint of a sneer. Borgia looked like he might eat a baby for lunch and enjoy every last morsel. Sam asked Leo about him, but whatever Leo knew, he was keeping to himself.

"He frightens you, doesn't he?" Sam asked.

"He is not a man to be trifled with. But frightened? Pah!" Then Leo grew serious. "I don't fear for myself, but I do fear for you."

One day, Borgia appeared out of nowhere. Unlike Leo's other friends, he never made a sound when he approached. It was as if his feet didn't quite touch the ground. He was dressed all in black. For the first time, he looked like the priest that he was. There was a gleam in his eye, as if he knew the answers to his questions before he asked them.

"What is this thing, Leonardo?"

Sam watched from behind a pile

of canvas. Borgia circled the machine, touching it here and there was he passed.

"It's my aerial screw, Your Grace. A flying machine."

"A flying machine. What fun." Borgia's voice dripped with contempt.

"Man dreams of flying, Your Grace. We must never give up on our dreams, even if they seem foolish."

"How true. You know, I have many dreams. I dream of becoming Pope. I dream of conquering all of Italy. Pope Cesare the Conqueror. Doesn't that have a nice ring?"

"If that's your dream." Leo was clearly unsettled.

"What I don't dream of is nonsense like this!" Borgia slammed his fist against one of the wooden struts, knocking it out of place and nearly breaking it. "This is not what I pay you for."

"Forgive me, Your Grace."

"Forgive you? I suppose it is in my power to forgive you. But I don't forgive you. I don't forgive traitors."

Leo looked shocked. "I have always been loyal to you."

"Really? When you spend my money and your time on children's toys, are you being loyal? I pay you to make maps, military maps, and military equipment. Is your studio full of maps? Is your workshop full of cannons? Not that I can see."

Leo didn't answer.

"I hear you have been seen with a young man." Cesare turned his head and looked directly at Sam. Sam shrunk down behind the canvasses.

"A young man?" Leo scoffed. "You mean Salai?

"I don't mean Salai. Everyone knows Salai. This is someone nobody knows."

Sam wondered where Salai was. He was always in the workshop, but today he was suspiciously absent.

"So many people come and go," Leo blustered. "Some delivery boy. Someone helping in the shop."

"Do I look like a fool? Don't treat me like a fool. Don't forget who supports you. The truth will come out, Leonardo. It always does." Cesare walked over to Leo and wiped his hands on Leo's cloak. Then he was gone.

Leo sat down hard. His face was pale, and beads of sweat dappled his forehead. Sam grabbed a bottle of wine and poured him a healthy glass. Leo drank it in one swallow.

"What did he mean when he said he supports you?" Sam asked.

"He does. He pays me for the work I do." Leo was still weak.

"So he's like your boss?" Sam was surprised

"He is my patron."

"Which means . . . ?" Sam asked.

"He provides me with materials to do my work. A place to live. Expenses for food, clothing." Leo looked sick, and suddenly very, very old.

"So this is his house. We're living in his house. He's not your boss! He's more like your master!" Leo had been warning him about Cesare, and all along they were living under his roof.

"No one masters Leonardo!"

"I don't believe this! What else haven't you told me!" Sam turned to go, to run anywhere, just to clear his mind.

But there was nowhere to run. Instead, there was Borgia and two armed guards.

"The truth always comes out, Leonardo." Borgia smiled.

ELEVEN

Trapped

Sam sat in the dark. He was mad. He was mad at Leo, he was mad at Borgia, he was mad at Salai. He was mad at the sixteenth century, he was mad at the Italian Renaissance. He was mad at Dylan, he was mad at Lurch and Burch, he was mad at himself for running through a stupid door that said "Keep Out" and falling through a stupid space-time portal into the stupid past. He was mad.

He didn't know what time it was, or how long he had been in the cell. He could check his phone, but he never reset the time when he fell into the past. Stupid phone. So he sat.

There was one small window, and a sliver of moon shone in to keep him company. Stupid moon. No, Sam decided, he couldn't be mad at the moon. It was his only friend left. It was the one thing that was the same here as it was at home. Except that there were no lunar rovers on it.

Then a light flickered, and a door opened. It was Borgia. Sam wondered why he knew that name. He remembered a Lucretia Borgia who poisoned, like, her whole family, but that's all he could come up with. And some cable TV show he didn't watch, because really, who wanted to watch a show about killer popes. Though putting it that way made it sound kind of cool.

"Let's have a chat."

"Great," thought Sam. At Millard Fillmore, those words were usually followed by a week's detention. Sam missed Fillmore.

"I must apologize for the accommodations," Borgia continued. "This home doesn't have a proper dungeon. I find these cells useful, though. Don't you?"

Sam was silent.

"Not up for a talk? You will be. I can keep you here for . . . how long? Forever, if I like. I dare not touch Leonardo. He has too many powerful friends. But a boy, especially a boy with no family? Boys go missing all the time." Borgia peered through the bars. Sam expected a forked tongue to snake out of his mouth at any moment.

"Leo won't let you keep me here." Sam's anger overrode his fear.

"Oh yes, 'Leo.' Leonardo will come to your rescue. What do you think he will do? Spirit you away in his famous flying machine? Break down the walls with his armored car? I suspect Leonardo is tucked into bed with a bottle of Madeira by now."

"He's twice the man you'll ever be!" Sam spat back.

"Ah, that's the fire I like to see!" Borgia gripped the bars of Sam's cell. "Yes, Leonardo is the greatest genius of our time—just ask him. There's only one problem with his inventions—they don't work. They're brilliant ideas, and lovely drawings, but nothing more. They're as likely to come to life as his Virgin Mary is to leap off the canvas and slap my face."

Sam seethed. He wouldn't give Borgia the pleasure of a reply.

"Who is the real genius? The man who finds the boy from the future, or the man who keeps him?"

Sam kept silent. What did Borgia know? How did he know it?

"You see, I have my genius too. Not for science, but for intrigue. I have eyes everywhere. A servant here, a merchant there. Perhaps an apprentice who favors money over loyalty."

"Salai!" Sam was hardly surprised.

"Indeed. He doesn't know much, unfortunately. Leonardo keeps his cards close. But what Salai knows, he's willing to share. As you will be in time."

"What do you want, *Borgia*?" Sam said the name as if it sickened him.

"That's Cardinal Borgia to you! Or Your Eminence, if you prefer." Sam glared at him. "I want everything. Everything you know. Access to the future. Who wouldn't want that?"

"I know one thing," said Sam. "In the future, the Borgias are known only for murder and betrayal."

"Really? How delightful. What about Della Rovere?"

"What's that?" Sam truly didn't know.

"The Cardinal of San Pietro," Borgia replied. "The pretender to the throne of Rome."

"I've never heard of him."

"Excellent!" Borgia laughed. "Better to be a famous villain than an unknown man of virtue. You will make our fortune, boy. Or rather increase it, since our fortune is already made many times over." Borgia turned to go.

"You can't leave me here," Sam called out.

"I can do whatever I wish. We'll chat again soon." Borgia swept from the room, taking the light with him.

Sam yelled. He cursed. He shook the bars of his cell. Anger was the only thing saving him from despair. But even anger passed in time. He was alone with the moon.

Then a figure entered the room. Was it Borgia, back for more? Or worse?

"Wake up, dung-breath. We're getting out of here."

TWELVE

Escape

"Salai!"

"Keep your voice down," Salai whispered. "You want the whole palace guard on our heels?"

"How did you get in here?" Sam whispered back.

"I have my ways." From his belt, Salai produced a ring of keys. He tried several in the lock of Sam's cell until he found one that worked. The door opened.

"Strong wine will get you most things you desire. A sleeping draught from Leonardo fills in the rest. Let's go." Salai started to move.

"Why should I trust you?" Sam asked. "I know you're working for Borgia."

"You want me to admit that I betrayed you to Borgia? Fine, I admit it. I was angry and stupid. I hated the way Leonardo treated you. We can fight about that here, or we can fight about it outside. I prefer outside."

"If you hate me, why are you helping me?" Sam still didn't trust Salai.

"I don't hate you. And for all his flaws, I love Leonardo. Besides, he says his goal is to send you back to where you came from. If that's the case, then he and I are united in our desire. Now let's go."

*   *   *   *   *

The young men crept through the palace. Sam could barely see, but Salai moved surely. Now and again they passed a guard station, but the guards were all sleeping. "That's the problem with being a Borgia," Salai whispered to Sam. "You don't really inspire a decent work ethic."

Eventually they came to a grate in the floor. Salai began to wrench it loose. "Hey kid, give me a hand."

"What are you doing?" Sam asked.

"Leonardo designed the drainage system for this dump. We're going down."

Sam helped with the grate. It was loose, but heavy. Finally it gave with a cry of twisted metal. Then there was a voice: "Halt! Stop where you are!"

It was a guard, his sword drawn. For a moment, no one moved. Then there was a flash of intense light. It blinded the guard, who reeled back and dropped his weapon. "Go," cried Sam, and in a heartbeat he and Salai were through the hole in the floor and down in the sewer below.

"What was that?" asked Salai.

Sam held up his phone. "Say cheese!"

THIRTEEN

Flight

Salai navigated the tunnels so well that Sam wondered how often he used them. When it seemed that they were lost, Sam used the light of his phone to help guide them. He kept the phone hidden in his underwear. "These sixteenth-century cops are rookies compared to what we've got back home. I guess my ass isn't as scrawny as Leo said," thought Sam. Then they were out.

Leo was waiting for them. Sam suppressed a cry when he saw the old man. Leo didn't bother. He grabbed Sam and pulled him into a bear hug.

"Yeah, happy ending, now let's get out of here," Salai cracked.

They rushed to the workshop, where the time machine was already loaded onto a cart. Two strong horses were harnessed to the front. "We worked through the night," Leo told Sam. "Salai was unstoppable. Unstoppable!"

"Come Leonardo, onto the cart. Kid, your stuff's in the back." Salai helped Leo into the cart while Sam jumped in the back. There was his backpack and his clothes. "Hyah!" cried Salai, and the cart began to move.

"Where are we going?" Sam asked from the back of the cart as he shucked out of his clothes. He was looking forward to getting back into his jeans.

"I plotted out the course of the portal

based on where we saw it last and how fast it was moving. I know precisely where we should find it."

"How precisely?" Sam asked.

"Eh," said Leo. "We hope for the best."

The horses were galloping now, and still Salai urged them on. "Borgia's men are slow to act, but their horses are swifter than ours," he explained. "Our only hope is to get away quickly."

Sam looked back. He thought he saw movement in the distance. "Hurry," he called.

On they charged. Sam felt the road rise. They were heading into higher ground. The wagon hit a bump, and the time machine inched backward.

"Be careful," he called up to Salai. "We're going to lose the machine."

"If we don't get to the top, we'll lose everything," he called back. "Do what you can."

"Do what I can," thought Sam. "I'm doing the best I can to not leap out of my skin."

He wedged his back against the machine and braced his feet against the edge of the cart. But try as he might, the machine kept slipping. In the distance, he definitely saw the dust of approaching horses. "Please hurry," he thought to himself. "Please please please."

"We're here!" Salai called out.

"Here" was the top of a steep rise. The road passed near the edge of a cliff. Too near for Sam's liking.

"We can't unload the machine," said Leo. "No time. We'll have to operate it from inside the cart. Sam, sit here and pedal. Salai and I will turn the cranks."

"Do I ride the machine back to the future?" asked Sam.

"No," said Leo. "The machine only opens the door. You pass through alone. Now pedal."

Sam pedaled. Leo and Salai turned the cranks. Slowly, the machine came to life. The canvas screw turned and flapped in the breeze. Two metal hoops spun and twirled, passing each other but never touching. The machinery spun and ground with a rhythmic *whoosh*, *whoosh*, *whoosh*. Sparks leapt between the hoops.

The horses were closer now. Sam could hear voices. Was that Borgia's, above them all?

"Look, Samuele! Behind you!"

Sam turned and looked, and there it was. The Door. Shimmering as it had in the field. But stronger now. Glowing, it seemed.

"You must go, Sam! Now!" Leo cried.

The horses grew closer. "Stop them!" called out Cesare Borgia.

Sam leapt from his seat. "Leo . . ."

"Just go!"

He grabbed his backpack and ran for the Door. It was moving. To the edge of the cliff.

"Go, Sam!"

"Jump, kid!"

"Stop him!"

Sam ran to the Door. It passed the edge of the cliff. He jumped.

And then he was falling.

FOURTEEN

Home

THUD!

"Am I dead?" thought Sam. He was face down in the dirt. He couldn't hear Leo, or Borgia, or the horses, or the machine.

"Hey kid, you okay?" Sam was definitely not okay. He rolled over and looked up.

A man stood on the cliff above him. Tall and angular, white-haired and clean-shaven.

"Leo?"

"Lenny, actually. Lenny Vincent, the custodian. Let me get a ladder."

Sam shook his head. It wasn't a cliff at all. It was an open doorway, the door he had run through back at Fillmore. He was sitting on the earth below, ten or twelve feet down. There was definitely a room above him, but the floor was torn up. "Danger. Keep Out," indeed.

He heard a roar. For a moment Sam thought it was Borgia and his men. Then he realized that no, it was just Dylan Matthews and the Goon Squad.

"Hey Shirley, stuck in a hole? Smooth move, Ex-Lax." Dylan laughed, and Lurch and Burch joined in. "When you get out of there, I'm still gonna kill you."

SMACK! Lenny had returned with the ladder, just in time to swat the back of Dylan's head. "No one's gonna kill nobody." He lowered the ladder into the hole and Sam climbed out.

"I'm not afraid of you, Dylan," Sam

said, and it was true. After spending a night in prison, being chased by soldiers, and falling through a space-time portal not once but *twice*, Dylan Matthews was no longer a threat.

"Oh yeah? I'll give you something to be afraid of."

"Not anymore. 'Cause I met a guy who taught me not to be afraid." Sam looked at Dylan as if he were one of Leo's bats. He was a typical bully. "You're just another kid trying to make it through a bad day. You're big and clumsy and you never pick on kids your own size. You know why? 'Cause you're afraid. You're afraid of what'll happen in a fair fight. So you pick on little kids 'cause they won't fight back. Well you don't scare me anymore."

Dylan roared. He threw himself at Sam, but Sam dodged out of the way. Sam knew one more thing that Dylan didn't. Behind him there was a door marked "Danger."

Dylan flew through the open door. There was a crash and an "Ooof!" as he landed on the earth below. Lurch and Burch couldn't help themselves. They burst into guffaws.

"I told you, I'm not afraid of you."

Epilogue

Sam's phone was dead. Whether it was the fall or the time machine or just one too many trips through the space-time portal, the SIM card was fried. Sam's pictures of Leo and the time machine were gone forever. Not that anyone would have believed his story anyway.

Things went back to normal at MFHS. Dylan Matthews kept his distance, and Sam kept his mouth shut. Nobody needed to know what had happened between them.

Sam read up on Leo and Borgia. He was happy to learn that Salai had made a somewhat scandalous name for himself.

Sam and Lenny became friends. Lenny had his own workshop, and Sam liked hanging out and helping out. Lenny was happy for a second pair of hands, and for someone who wasn't afraid of hot solder and power tools. One day Sam turned to Lenny and asked, "Hey, Lenny. You ever think about making a time machine?"

"Funny you should mention it," Lenny answered.

But that's another story.